a raft
around the corner

and other stories to keep you going

david pippenger

HandCrafted Media Press

Published by
HandCrafted Media Press
A wholly owned division of
HandCrafted Media Ltd.
481 Highway 105, Suite B-108
Monument, Colorado 80132
(719-481-8200)

Composition by Greenleaf Book Group LP

ISBN: 0-9767613-0-0
Library of Congress Control Number: 2005930619
Printed in the United States of America
10 9 8 7 6 5 4 3 2 1
www.araftaroundthecorner.com

From the dawn of time there have been stories. Stories told around the campfire or when children went to bed. Stories told at times of celebration and ritual, when people were frightened or insecure. Stories told to reminisce, to share personal experiences, to impart gems of wisdom, to entertain, for protection, to treasure generational inheritance, to maintain oral tradition, and to increase bonding between family and friends. The great philosophers, prophets, poets, writers and visionaries were quintessential storytellers. Remnants of their craft exist today, often in the form of fairy tales, allegories, and myth.

Life is a three-dimensional story that *you* live. Your story differs from anyone else's on this planet. Because of that, you always have something to share, just as you always have something to learn. Within your life story are myriad short stories that reflect what you did, where you went, what you saw, who you spent time with, what you accomplished, what mistakes you made, what lessons you learned (or didn't learn) and what contributions you made on your life journey.

Stories are powerful! A good story can enter your memory easily and may still be there decades later. Those who ignore the importance of story and metaphor do so at their own peril. The human brain—at almost any age, in every culture and in every era—loves stories. In fact, the brain is designed to process them. Tiny organs within the emotional layer of the brain are highly attuned to symbolic meanings that come to it through story and metaphor.

Stories form the basic fabric for intelligence because they help determine how you think and behave. They can help you make sense of the world, relax, reduce stress and heal. They can give life to past experiences, present situations and even to the future. In fact, you often dream in story format.

Stories have been found to play a special role in the development of memory, attention and reflective thought patterns. They can foster a love for words and a facility with language and bring ideas to life. They can instill character, education and convey information without seeming to do so. They can arouse emotion, which is key for learning.

Stories can reach and educate both heart and mind. They can stimulate active mental picturing (as compared to passive picturing that is honed through viewing television and videos) and develop your imagination, an ability that is utilized in a wide range of intellectual activities and required for all types of problem solving. They can offer you a way to look at something from a more objective perspective, especially when a sensitive or problematic area needs to be addressed.

With the advent of 20th century technology and beyond, storytelling—the pure unadulterated sharing of stories with another for the sheer joy of the telling and the listening—sometimes gets left behind in the plethora of sound, sight and sensation. But the art of storytelling is not lost. It still exists. It's just waiting for you to take it from the shelf, dust it off and access its elegant power to connect and resonate with the human spirit.

This book of 21st century stories is a great way to begin. Each one has its genesis in a real happening. Read them. Ponder them. Learn from them. Have fun with them. Allow your brain to luxuriate in them. Share them with others. Soak up the benefits they can provide. Make them part of your life story in your very own way!

Arlene Taylor, Ph.D.
Brain Function Specialist
www.arlenetaylor.org

This is a book
        of stories
                that can help you keep going
                        when things aren't going well.
This is a book
        of stories
                that can be re-told when things get better.

But most importantly . . .

This is a book
        of stories
                that can be *remembered*
                      when things aren't going well . . .
                                the next time.

David Pippenger

Henry Ford once said, "Failure is only the opportunity to begin again more intelligently."

In other words: As long as you don't give up, failure can be an essential part of success.

As strange as it sounds, failure should lead to confidence. After all, when you fail, you know something you didn't know before.

OK, I know that's a stretch for most people.

Perhaps that's because most of the time, the confidence that people exude is only a reflection of the external situation around them and not the glow of internal knowledge.

When things are going well, confidence swells.

When things are not going well, confidence dips.

So here is something for you to think about: External confidence relies on the world around you to exist. Internal confidence relies on no one for its existence, except you.

External confidence is a reflection; internal confidence is a light.

Internal light (confidence) is the essence of being positive.

But lights are funny things. They can burn out, fade over time, or stop working completely if the power is deficient.

Sometimes the switch is just turned off.

It is my hope that the stories in this book will provide you with the ability to connect, or if necessary, reconnect, recharge or just plain flip the switch on to the power of internal confidence.

David Pippenger

Dedicated to Richard and Lindsay.

Wonderful friends who have stayed positive,
amid unbearable sorrow.

During a late night discussion that included a lot of what is in this book, a friend looked me in the eye and said, "You really need to get this written down."

So I did.

That friend was Larry Hargrave. Without his encouragement these words would have stayed inside my head and never made the transition to print.

Then it dawned on me . . . I had lots of words to write, but I didn't have any letters after my name (and therefore, no credentials). I called the person with more letters after her name than anybody I knew (four degrees including two doctorates), Dr. Arlene Taylor. She liked the concept of this book enough to say she would make sure I didn't make an idiot out of myself (at least as far as this book was concerned). Arlene has been a close friend for years, and having her as a resource is something for which I will always be grateful.

After the words were a reality, I needed to make sure they were in the right order. For that I have my daughter Sarah to thank. I also need to thank her husband CJ, who gave up time with his wife so that she could edit this book.

To my son Jonathan, thanks for the encouragement on the early editions. I can think of no better philosopher to bounce ideas off. Also, thanks for letting me write a couple of stories about you (you know which ones they are).

After a worldwide search for an illustrator, I was ecstatic when Greg Mathieson sent me a sample of his work. Each of his illustrations captures the essence of the story with amazing simplicity and beauty. Greg's contribution to this work can only be described as absolutely phenomenal.

There are a host of others who have provided invaluable assistance at key times. Thank you.

Most importantly, I wish to thank my wife Joy.

Joy, you are more precious to me than the air that I breathe. Every day I thank God for over a quarter century of the most amazing days any man could ever hope for.

Contents

A Raft Around the Corner 1

The Emotional Scale 7

The Game is Longer Than You Think 15

Against the Current 21

Move On 33

Give In to the Positive 53

Soaked With Sadness 59

A Raft in the City 65

Strike Two 71

The First Eight Balls Don't Count 79

You Have to Give Up Something To Get Something 85

Can Fear Change the Weather? 105

Life Is a Movie 115

Postscript 127

ONE | a raft around the corner

"Of course truth is stranger than fiction.
Fiction has to make sense."

—Mark Twain

This is a true story . . .

Albeit, the short version.

A man found himself floating down the rapids in a river at the bottom of a canyon, miles from anywhere, in the middle of a wilderness area with his ankle broken in half.

Having been trained on to how to get out of the rapids, he determined that he would get to the shore, and he did.

Not having been trained in what to do with a broken ankle in the bottom of a canyon . . . he determined that he would walk out of the canyon and up the steep, rocky path just as he had come down.

He did not.

You see, his ankle had the deciding vote, and it had decided that walking up a rocky slope was not in its best interest.

So, in an effort to appease the broken ankle,
        the man tried to walk

using a crutch made from a tree.

Which was a brilliant idea . . .

If he had been walking on a smooth sidewalk
going downhill
for a short distance.

But he wasn't.

He was next to a river at the bottom of a canyon, miles from anywhere, in the middle of a wilderness area with his ankle broken in half.

So he decided to think of every possible solution and choose the best one.

From helicopters to climbing teams, he imagined every possible means to get out of the canyon that was miles from anywhere, in the middle of a wilderness area—with his ankle broken in half.

But while he was thinking,

a raft came around the corner.

Which was interesting,
because even though he had tried to think
of every possible solution . . .

he never thought of a raft.

But that wasn't all.

Because in the raft was a Wilderness Emergency Medical Technician.

Which was particularly interesting, because the man with the broken ankle didn't know there *was* such a thing as a Wilderness Emergency Medical Technician and he certainly didn't expect one to be on a raft that he hadn't even thought of.

Well, the Wilderness EMT made a splint with duct tape and branches from a tree and put the man in his raft, and later that night they camped at a beautiful spot on the river and ate chicken fajitas and strawberry shortcake.

Which was interesting, because the man with the broken ankle thought that he would be eating the dehydrated eggs that he had in his backpack.

Then he realized

that a lot of things he hadn't thought of
        and a lot of things that he *had* thought of
                had turned out
    in ways
                that he never thought of.

Which is why I am telling you this story.

I was the man with the broken ankle.

And that day
>next to a river
>>at the bottom of a canyon,
>>>miles from anywhere
>>>>in the middle of a wilderness area
>>>>>with my ankle broken in half . . .

I learned that I could not possibly imagine all of the amazing things that were in store for me in my life.

Proust says that we shouldn't look for new vistas, but instead look with fresh eyes.

He's right.

No matter what life is throwing at us, there is a raft around the corner that we cannot see.

Don't look for it;
>it cannot be seen.

Don't predict when it will appear;
>it's not on your timetable.

Don't doubt that it exists,
>for doubt will cloud your eyes
>>and cause you
>>>to give up before it arrives.

Don't give up;

give in.

Give in to the idea that positive events are in your future, even if you can't see them.

Give in to the idea that positive events are in your future, even if you can't imagine what they could possibly be.

There's a raft around the corner.

Don't limit yourself to what you know.

Or, to say it positively . . .

There are more options available to you than you can possibly imagine.

TWO | the emotional scale

"Children must be taught how to think,
not what to think."

—Margaret Mead

Luke loved to climb trees.

The bigger, the better.

His mother has a picture of him when he was only four-years old, at the top of a very tall tree, hugging the trunk as if his life depended on it.

Well, actually, his life did depend on it.

As small as he was, as high as he was, the weight of his body caused the treetop to sway back and forth like a metronome. As young as he was, he loved being able to make that big tree move.

As scared as she was, his mom let him do it.

Some of the neighbors thought she was a terrible mom for letting Luke climb to the top of a very tall tree.

To Luke, she was a great mom.

After a little bit, Luke's mom would call up to him and tell him to climb down to a bigger branch. Regretfully, he would do it, and the swaying would stop.

There, in the safety of the branches, he could feel his heart settle down from the rapid drum beat it had escalated to while at the very top of the swaying tree. He would shake his hands and let some of the blood move back into his fingers. When he was at the very top and hanging on for his life, he would hold on so tight that sometimes his hands would tingle like they were going to sleep.

He never told his mom that.

He didn't have to. She had climbed a few trees herself when she was young and knew exactly what Luke was feeling.

In fact, she still had scar on the back of her shoulder from the time when she fell out of a very tall tree.

As much as it hurt when she fell, she knew she couldn't spend her life keeping Luke from feeling the same pain. That's why she let Luke climb trees like she did.

She really was a great mom.

To Luke, the tree was more than a tree; it was a friend, a confidant and a refuge. When he was sitting on the last big branch just below the top of the tree, he was happy. Sure he loved to climb up and get a tingle up his spine from being at the very top, but without the big branch to sit on, he had to hold on so tight that he would eventually either have to scoot back down to the last big branch or he would risk losing his grip and falling all the way to the bottom.

When he was sitting on the last big branch, he could see the whole range of mountains that were visible from his perch but were invisible from the yard.

Like I said, he was happy.

Luke's mom learned a lot from the tree.

When Luke was angry, he would never climb up to the last big branch. He would stop in a bare section of the tree just below his favorite perch and yell into the wind.

When he was afraid, he would only climb a bit off the ground and hide in a thicket of branches that were so dense he couldn't be seen.

When he was sad, he wouldn't climb the tree at all. He would just sit at the trunk of the tree and lean against it. With his back against the tree, he would push against the trunk with all of his might. Unlike when he was at the top, the tree never moved. Being around such a solid object made him feel better.

If things were really going bad in his life, he wouldn't go outside at all. When his mom encouraged him to turn off the television and go climb his tree, he would respond that he didn't care about the tree.

Watching Luke climb trees didn't scare his mom, but watching Luke sit and stare at the TV scared her to death.

So she always found a way to get him back up in the tree.

Like I said, she was a great mom.

Eventually, Luke grew up and his taste for adventure outgrew the tree.

As a teenager, when he needed to feel the tingle up his spine, he would take his bike up on the roof of his house and with the same grip that he used to hold on to the tree, he would hold on to the handlebars of his bike and ride it off the roof, onto the garage and then to the shed and finally with a loud "thud" land in the yard. When he broke the frame of his bike doing this, his mom didn't tell him to stop . . . she bought him a stronger bike.

She told him that even though she never jumped off a building on a bike when she young, she did get a bully to stop bothering her younger brother by riding like the wind on her little bike until she was able to put a stick in the bully's spokes.

She wasn't sure what was more surprising to the bully—the fact that this skinny little girl could ride faster than he could, or the fact that he was flying over his handles and into the dirt because she stuck a stick in his spokes.

The bully's bike, as well as the bully himself, was never the same.

Years later, in high school, when Luke's mom agreed to go out on a date with the (former) bully, he admitted that he fell in love with her the day he fell off of his bike—with her help.

Six years after that, on the day they got married, Luke's mom admitted she only went out with him when they were in high school because she felt bad about knocking him off his bike.

Luke learned a lot from his mom.

Luke's mom learned a lot from his bike.

Sure, there were times when he jumped off of buildings and over fences, but usually, when he was happiest, he would take his bike up into the mountains and just ride. He would be gone for a very long time and come home with a contented grin on his face. It was as if he could ride like that forever.

His mom loved those days.

When he was angry, he would ride into the wind and yell just like he did at the top of the tree when he was four-years old.

When he was afraid, he would get on his bike and ride as fast as he could for as long as he could, which wasn't very long. It takes a lot of energy to be afraid.

When he was sad, he would just sit on his bike and not ride it at all.

And when he told his mom he didn't care if he ever rode his bike again, she knew something was very, very wrong.

So she found a way to get him back on his bike, and back on the long rides in the mountains where he was happiest.

Like I said, she was a very good mom.

Years later, when Luke and his mom stood next to each other and watched Luke's own son climb a rock wall, Luke commented on how she let him experience so many things, but always seemed to get him back to where he was happiest.

"I loved to see you happy."

"But I wasn't always happy," he said.

"Nobody is," came her reply.

"So it didn't bother you when I was unhappy?"

"It never bothered me when you were angry, afraid or sad . . . It only bothered me when you stayed there, or worse, when you didn't care."

"So what did you do?" Luke asked as he watched his son miss a handhold and fall a few feet until his rope tightened and pulled him against the wall.

"Nothing," came her reply.

He looked at her surprised, "Nothing?"

"Not a thing," she said with a smile. "I had confidence in you."

Luke looked at his mom with astonishment in his eyes.

"You got me back up in the tree or back on my bike without doing anything?"

"Nothing at all."

There was a long pause as Luke stood there and shook his head. He knew she did something.

He tried to remember what she said, or what she did that always got him back to the place he was happiest.

Then he smiled.

He remembered.

"You didn't do anything except give me confidence in myself . . . because you had confidence in me."

Then he wrapped his long, strong arms around her and gave her a hug just like he hugged that tree in the picture when he was four-years old.

For a long time they just stood there, hugging.

She always let the child decide when the hug was over.

Like I said, she was a great mom.

You can't do better than to encourage others
to believe in themselves.

Or, to say it positively . . .

Look for the positive in others . . .
and then let them know you have confidence in them.

THREE 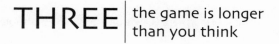 the game is longer than you think

"It is just the little touches after the average man would quit that make the master's fame."

—Orison Swett Marden

It has been said about a world famous athlete: He never lost a game, he just ran out of time.

That's the way games are.

They have a beginning and an end.

Some games are played by the clock.
Some are played until a certain score is reached.
Some are played for a certain number of plays.

But they all end.

And usually there is a winner and a loser, although some games end in a tie . . .

>which means nobody wins
>and everybody loses.

At least that's what it feels like to the people who are used to winning.

Even for the people who are used to losing, they know that a tie is still not a win, because only a win is a win . . . and everybody loves to win.

Conversely, nobody likes to lose.

It's hard to be positive about losing.

Sure, you can talk about the next game, the next season, the next whatever . . . but it doesn't take the sting out of losing.

Just ask that world famous athlete mentioned above.

You see, there was a time when the world famous athlete was known as a loser.

Not by everyone.

Not even by most.
But there were *some* who enjoyed pulling down a man who was in the stratosphere of fame and fortune.

No matter how many games he came from behind to win, no matter how many division championships he orchestrated, no matter how many records he broke . . . according to some, he was a loser.

That's what people call you when you end every season with a loss.

Only champions end the season with a win.

He was not a champion.

That meant he was a loser . . . to some people.

For fourteen years he watched the winners walk off of the field.
For fourteen years all he could talk about after the last game was the next season.
For fourteen years he would pick up the newspapers with his picture on the front page next to the word "loser."

Well, the paper actually just used the word "loss" to describe the game . . . but to those who think winning is everything, they might as well have said, "loser."

It had to be hard not to give up.

He had enough money.
He had enough fame.
He had enough of everything . . .

Except winning.

That's because champions are champions long before they are actually *champions*. And this champion wanted to walk off the field a winner.

So he kept playing.

Then, one year, he found himself with the right coaches, the right teammates and the right experience to end the season with a win. The newspapers proclaimed him a winner.

Then it happened again the next year.

Now he was a *proven* winner.

Then those same people who called him a loser, now called him their champion.

And he was gracious enough to let them, because his game, the *real* game, had no time limits.

All he had to do was keep playing until he won.

Which is why the game is longer than you think.

You see, it's not just one game,
        or just one season
                or even one lifetime.

The game is longer than you think . . .

keep playing.

The only time we draw our own finish line is when we quit.

Or, to say it positively . . .

In the game of life, there's always another game.

FOUR | against the current

"We have been taught to believe that negative equals realistic and positive equals unrealistic."
—Susan Jeffers

Once upon a time, there was a cute young frog that found herself in the middle of a very fast-moving river.

Normally, the frog liked to travel in fast water because she liked to get places fast, but on this day she did not like where the water was taking her.

It was taking her out to sea.

Fast.

The problem was that all along the shores of the river there were hungry crocodiles.

Now, a frog isn't much of a meal to a hungry crocodile, but when you're hungry, even a small meal is better than none, so all of the crocodiles were smacking their lips and hoping the frog would swim their way. (Fortunately for the frog, these crocs were lazy as well as hungry, which meant they didn't want to chase after a little frog, since it really wasn't much of a meal after all.)

The frog, on the other hand, was doing her best to stay away from the shore since she didn't really like the idea of being a crocodile snack.

Well, actually, she didn't like the idea of being a snack at all, no matter who did the snacking. Which is why she didn't like the idea of being washed into the sea.

In the sea, a cute young frog was no longer a snack, but a full-course meal. At least that was what the wisest, oldest frog in her pond told her during a lecture at the lily pad school.

As she sat and listened to the lecture, she found herself NOT thinking about the creatures in the sea, but instead how the wise old frog *got* AWAY from the creatures in the sea, if they were really so intent on eating him.

So she raised her hand politely and asked him.

The wise old frog cleared his throat (as wise old frogs are prone to do) and said that he himself had never seen the sea or the sea creatures, which was evident since he was in the classroom and not in the belly of the sea creatures, but it was in fact his grandfather who had been to the sea, and it was he who had told him about the sea creatures.

Well the wise old frog thought he had answered the young frog's question, but the young frog raised her hand again.

"Yes?" he asked the young frog.

"Wouldn't it be better for you to teach us how your grandfather got away from the sea creatures, just in case we somehow ended up in the sea, rather than just tell us not to go to the sea?"

At that point the wise old frog sent the young frog to the back of the lily pad and never called on her again.

Which is where the young frog wished she were right now: Safely sitting at the back of the lily pad with all of her friends.

But she wasn't.

She was floating down a river past hungry crocodiles into a sea filled with sea creatures that wanted to eat her for lunch. Or dinner. Or breakfast. She didn't really know since frogs don't wear wristwatches.

What she *did* know was that there were a lot of very big teeth grinning at her from all around.

Which caused her to scold herself.

"Why didn't you get on that old tree like you always do?"

She said this because up the river, between the crocodiles and the wise old frog, there was a tree that had fallen into the river.

A very big tree with lots of twisted branches.

Not only was it a perfect log for a frog to get out of the river before reaching the crocodiles and the sea, but with all of those twisted branches it was also great protection from birds with sharp claws that liked to grab frogs and hoist them high up into the sky.

She didn't know what the birds did after they hoisted frogs high up into the sky, but she was sure it wasn't good.

She decided to ask the wise old frog that question the next time she was in the back of the lily pad with her friends.

That is, *if* she ever got back to the lily pad.

But today, instead of jumping onto the tree with the twisted branches that would keep her from floating out to sea and protect her from the birds with sharp claws that hoisted frogs high up into the sky, the cute young frog decided to see what was beyond the tree—for no other reason than she had never before seen what was beyond the tree.

She had heard about it, but she had never seen it for herself.

At the time, that seemed like a good enough reason.

Only now that she was seeing it for herself,
she wished she wasn't seeing it.

But wishing was not going to get her back to the tree . . .

> and hope was not going to get her past the
> crocodile's teeth,

> and all the positive thoughts in the world
> were not going to stop that river
> from washing her
> out to sea.

At least that was what the wise old frog had said.

She decided not to think about the wise old frog anymore.

So she tried to think of what *could* save her from being eaten by
crocodiles or washed out to sea.

She immediately came up with a solution. "I will have to work
harder," she decided.

That was it. If she swam as hard as she possibly could, then she
could get back to the big tree with the twisted limbs.

She looked upstream for the big tree to see how far she would have to swim, but the current had taken her so far she couldn't see it.

She decided she didn't have to see it. She knew it was there and she knew it was safe. All she had to do was get there.

She looked over at a big ugly crocodile on the shore who was staring at her through one eye.

He only used one eye because where the other eye should have been, there was just an ugly scar.

"He probably lost his other eye trying to fight off the other crocodiles when they were all trying to eat my great-great-grand relative," she thought.

Then she decided to use that ugly old one-eyed croc as a marker.

"When that old croc is far behind me, I will know the big tree with the twisted limbs is close."

And with that, she started swimming.

Hard.

She even closed her eyes so that she could be surprised at the great distance she had put between herself and the one-eyed croc.

She swam and she swam and she swam.

Then she opened her eyes.

And sure enough, she was amazed at the distance she had put between herself and the one-eyed croc.

Except, she was amazed that there *wasn't* any distance between her and the one-eyed croc.

The current was so strong that she had been swimming in place.

So she stopped swimming.

"All is lost," she thought to herself as she got so close to the sea that she could smell the salt in the air.

"No, all is not lost," she said back to herself.

"I have never seen a sea creature, so it is possible that none of them exist," she said with a very optimistic tone.

Then a barracuda swam by the mouth of the river.

The young frog looked at the long powerful body of the fish and was immediately afraid.

"What are you afraid of?" she asked herself. "You don't even know if he has teeth."

As if hearing her thoughts, the barracuda smiled an enormous smile that showed what must have been a thousand very sharp teeth.

"OK, so he has teeth," the cute young frog said out loud. "But he's probably not even hungry."

"Are you kidding?" said a crab nearby in disbelief. "Do you think he got to be that size by *not* eating? He's *always* hungry."

The frog had never had a crab talk to her before, but today was a day of firsts, so it didn't surprise her.

"Well, then I choose to believe that he doesn't like to eat frogs," the young frog said with all of the hope she had left.

"You can choose to believe all you want, but I happen to know that frogs are his favorite dish," said the crab in a very crabby voice.

"But I'm the only frog here . . . and there are *lots* of crabs. Why would he prefer just *one* frog over a *plate full* of crabs?" asked the frog defensively.

"Look at this!" the crab said, waving around his claws. My skeleton is on the *outside* of my body, but you're all soft and squishy. Which would *you* rather eat?"

The frog did have to admit that the crab had a point.

"You might as well give up."

"You mean there's nothing I can do?" asked the cute young frog.

"Nope," replied the crab.

"Can *you* help me?"

"I can't even walk straight."

"What does that have to do with helping me out of a river?

"I don't know. It's just how I answer everything."

"So you're a pessimist," said the frog.

"I'm a realist," replied the crab.

"What does that mean?" asked the frog.

"It means that you got yourself into this mess and you've thought and hoped and tried everything, but none of it has worked—so you might as well just accept the fact that you are going to be eaten, no matter how optimistic you are."

"But I'm *not* optimistic," answered the frog emphatically. "I see the same things you do, and I don't see any way out either."

"OK then, be a good realist and give up," said the crab in a way that proved his point.

"I would, but I don't believe I'm smart enough to have thought of everything," the frog said reflectively.

"What does *that* mean?" asked the crab as he scratched his head with a big claw.

"You said that I've thought and hoped and tried *everything*."

"It's true," answered the crab. "I've been watching you and you've tried everything, but none of it has worked."

"Do *I* have to think of something for it to work?" asked the frog.

The crab used two claws to scratch his head and said, "You're giving me a headache."

"What I'm saying is—yes, I have tried everything I can think of, but I'm only a frog. There have to be a lot of possibilities that can happen even if I can't think of them."

"Name one," replied the crab.

"I can't. That's the point."

"Can you blow up into a ball and look bigger than you really are?" asked the crab.

"No."

"Can you spit poison?"

"No."

"Well, that's all I can think of," said the crab with finality.

"Thanks for trying," said the frog politely.

"Hey, I heard about a frog who could make poison come out of his eyes . . . maybe you're one of those?!" said the crab with as much optimism as a realistic crab could muster.

"What good will that do?" asked the frog incredulously.

The crab thought for a minute then said, "When the barracuda licks your eye, he'll die!"

"Why would a barracuda lick my eye?" asked the frog.

The crab didn't know that frogs asked so many questions.

"Well, maybe you have to kind of lean in a direction that makes your eye look like something he likes to lick," said the crab as he leaned forward with his eye bulging.

"That doesn't make me want to lick your eye," said the frog matter-of-factly.

"Hey, this is *your* game, I'm just trying to play along," said the crab in a way that let the frog know she had hurt his feelings.

"But it *is* something I hadn't thought of," said the frog, trying to cheer up the crab, "which proves my point that there *are* things that can happen that I haven't thought of."

"Well if they're all as good as *that* idea, they will prove *my* point," replied the crab in his crabby voice.

"What point is that?" asked the frog.

"You're toast," said the crab.

"Oh," replied the frog.

Just then the cute young frog tasted something she had never tasted before.

"What is that?" she asked as she spit out the water.

"What is what?" asked the crab.

"The water in this river tastes funny," said the frog.

The crab stuck out his tongue and tasted the water.

"You're tasting salt water," said the crab. "We're in the estuary."

"What's an estuary?" asked the frog.

"It's where the sea and the river meet," answered the crab in a way that showed the frog that he was proud of himself for knowing the answer.

"But we aren't to the sea shore yet!" said the frog as she looked down the last bit of the river.

"We don't have to be. About every six hours the current changes."

"You mean . . ."

"This river is going into reverse," said the crab.

"A river that goes both directions? I never knew that such a thing was even possible!" said the frog in amazement.

"It happens so many times around here, I don't even notice it," said the crab as the current pushed him slightly upstream.

The frog looked at the current and exclaimed, "Does that mean I'm going back up the river?"

"What are you so excited about? It's no big deal . . . It happens about every six hours—or weren't you listening?" asked the crab in a huff.

"Look!" the frog said as she floated away from the crab "I'm not going to be washed out to sea!" said the frog almost in disbelief. "I'm not going to be eaten by the barracuda!"

The crab rubbed his chin and said, "Guess not."

Then he smiled and said, "At least not today," which convinced the frog that crabs are only happy when things are going bad.

But she didn't care because now she was heading back to the tree with the twisted limbs and the lily pad where all her friends were.

"And to think I worked so hard trying to swim back to the tree, when now the current is going to take me back up the river all by itself," she said, as she kicked effortlessly upstream in the salty current.

"Well, technically, if you hadn't swum in place for so long, you would have been in the belly of that barracuda when the current changed," mused the crab.

"So hard work pays off even when it doesn't?" asked the frog.

The crab rubbed his head again. "Now you're giving my headache a headache," he said with a painful look on his face.

"Goodbye," said the frog as she waved at the crab and floated toward home.

"Goodbye," said the crab as he waved one of his big claws at the disappearing frog.

Which just happened to catch the eye of the barracuda.

Don't worry when your hard work
doesn't look like it's paying off.

Or, to say it positively . . .

Do your best and the results will take care of the rest.

> "The whole point of being alive
> is to evolve into the complete person
> you were intended to be."
> —Oprah Winfrey

Jay was a guy who wanted things to make sense.

He didn't want a million dollars, a fancy job or the applause of the crowd . . .
>
> he just wanted the crowd
> to make sense.

Jay spent a lot of time thinking.

When he was thinking, he was usually thinking about how to make sense out of things that didn't make sense.

Now, if you're thinking that *thinking* about making sense out of things that don't make sense is a frustrating job . . .
>
> you're right.

Jay knew that sometimes things didn't make sense, but he just figured it was because he hadn't thought hard enough.

That was not the case.

Jay thought hard enough for ten people.

Because
all he wanted was for things to make sense.

And sometimes they didn't.

Like today.

Three-quarters of the way through a series of tests that would determine what he would do for the rest of his life, Jay found himself in an empty white room, sitting at a table staring at a piece of paper, a puzzle and two small metal containers. One container was red, the other blue.

The piece of paper had a short title at the top that said:

Instructions:

At least *that* made sense.

Every other test had come with the same piece of paper that had the same title in the same font in the same place.

Jay usually liked things to be different, but after spending an eternity taking these tests, he was glad for a little familiarity.

Under the title were the simple instructions:

"After you have finished with the puzzle, proceed through the door on your left. If you do not wish to continue with the testing, proceed through the door to your right."

Jay wondered if there was any significance to the fact that the door to continue was on the left when most people were right-handed.

Like I said, Jay thought enough for ten people.

He also wondered what was in the small metal containers.
Picking up the blue container, he noticed a thin line around the circumference. A closer look revealed that the line was actually a very thin gap that went completely around the container.

"It's a lid." Jay said out loud.
He pulled on the lid and the metal container opened.

There was nothing inside.

Which didn't make sense.

Why have a container with nothing in it?

Jay looked the container over carefully.

It appeared to be made of aluminum or thin steel and had no identifying marks or labels other than the blue paint that covered the outside completely.
Jay put the top back on, and then easily removed it again with a gentle tug. This action was interesting to Jay since the top and bottom fit together very tightly.

The red metal container caught his eye.

Putting down the blue container, Jay picked up the red container.

A close examination revealed that this container also had a thin line around the circumference, although it appeared to have a wider gap than the blue container.

Jay wondered why the last person who took this test didn't put the lid on tightly.

Jay *wondered* enough for ten people too.

Jay pulled on the lid just like he did on the blue container.

It didn't open.

Which made sense.

The larger gap on the red container wasn't there because the last person hadn't put the lid on tightly enough; it was there because it was *too* tight.

Jay worked at getting the lid off, but to no avail.

Out of habit, he shook the container next to his ear.

I say it was out of habit because as far back as anybody could remember, anytime Jay would try to figure something out, he would shake it next to his ear.

If you asked him *why* he did that, Jay would think about it for a while and then look at you and say, "I want to know if it makes any noise."

Which made sense.

To him.

Because what he was really saying was that he wanted to know if there was something more to the object than meets the eye.

In this case, the red metal container made no noise.

He tried to open it again, but the lid wouldn't budge.

He looked at the gap in the red container as close as he could, and noticed a small discoloration. He scraped at it with his fingernail and it came off.

"It's rusted shut." Jay said out loud again.

Jay almost always said things out loud when he was thinking.

If you asked him *why* he said things out loud when he was thinking, he would think about it for a bit and then say, "I like to hear the words."

Which made sense.

To him.

Because words that stayed in his head didn't really seem like words. But when he *heard* the words—even if he was the one saying them—*then* they seemed like words.

He gave the red container one last tug and then put it back down on the table.

Picking up the puzzle pieces, Jay noted that the pieces were made of a heavy, dark wood and formed into a variety of geometric shapes.

The pieces were three-dimensional and included a triangle, a ball, a rectangle, a square, a square with a hole in it, a larger triangle, a smaller square, a pyramid—and one piece that appeared to have bits and pieces of each of the other pieces carved out of its edges. Each piece was very smooth and was finished with what looked like a zillion coats of hand-rubbed varnish.

Jay rubbed his thumb along the side of the rectangle.

Jay always rubbed smooth things with his thumb.

If you asked him *why* he rubbed smooth things with his thumb, he would think about it and then answer, "Because it feels good."

Which made sense.

To everybody.

Because smooth objects *do* feel good when you rub them with your thumb.

Putting down the rectangle, Jay picked up the odd-shaped piece that had the other shapes carved out of its edges and said out loud in a quiet singing voice, "You're a mean one . . . Mr. Grinch."

Which meant that this was an important object.

Nobody needed to ask Jay why he said that, since everybody knew he loved Dr. Seuss.

Jay put down the odd-shaped piece and then looked at all of the items on the table . . . and thought about them.

Then he picked up the odd-shaped piece and turned it over in his hand.

As he looked at each of the edges, Jay hummed the tune that went along with the words, "You're a mean one, Mr. Grinch . . ." He stopped when he got to what looked like a pyramid-shaped hole carved into one side. Picking up the small pyramid, he fit the piece snugly into the place that matched the shape on the odd-shaped piece.

He was surprised to see that the piece fit so precisely that all that could be seen of the pyramid was the outline of the base. The pyramid itself was completely inside the odd-shaped piece.

He tapped the odd-shaped piece gently on the table to knock the pyramid shape back out, but it didn't budge.

He picked up the rectangle piece, looked at it and then turned the odd-shaped piece around until he found a spot that matched the shape.

Just like the pyramid, the rectangle slid into the spot perfectly.

Also like the pyramid, Jay could not remove the piece once it had been put in place.

That didn't make sense.

How were the pieces locking into place?

Jay picked up the pieces one by one and examined them. There were no locks or grooves on any of them.

Jay thought about it for quite a while and then determined that there must be a very strong magnet inside the odd-shaped piece and a corresponding piece of metal inside each object.

He tested his theory by placing the red metal container next to the odd-shaped piece and letting go of it.

Sure enough, the metal container stayed attached to the odd-shaped piece.

Which made sense, since the spot of rust meant that the container was made of some ferrous material and ferrous material would be attracted to a magnet.

Jay liked it when things made sense.

He quickly inserted each of the other pieces into their corresponding niches within the odd-shaped piece.
Each time, he would slide the piece in slowly and marvel at the precision and preciseness of the puzzle.

He was a bit stymied by the marble, since there were no round shapes on the edge of the odd-shaped piece . . . but then he placed the marble inside the hole of the cube and it fit perfectly. He then slid both pieces into the odd-shaped piece, where they stayed just like all of the other pieces.

Well, all of the other pieces except one.

Because there wasn't a piece . . . only a trapezoidal hole for it to go into.

Which didn't make sense.

Why would they give him a puzzle without all the pieces?

He looked on the floor to see if he had knocked any pieces off of the table.

Nope. No pieces were on the floor.

He stood up and brushed at his clothing to see if a piece had gotten lost in the folds of his shirt or pants.

Nope. No pieces were there either.

He looked around the room trying to see if someone had hidden a piece on the ledge of the door.

Nope. No pieces were in the room.

This was very frustrating.

He was tired and he wanted to go home, but the only way he could go home was to finish the puzzle or quit the test and he certainly didn't want to quit the test when he was three-quarters of the way through. But he couldn't finish the puzzle without the last piece.

This was *very* frustrating.

So he sat down and thought about it.

Then he thought about it some more.

Then he thought about the red container.

Holding it up to the spot where the missing piece would go, he decided that it was possible for the missing piece to be inside the metal container.

He shook it next to his ear.

There was still no sound.

He picked up the blue container, put the lid back on it and held it in his right hand. He then picked up the red container and held it in his left hand.

"They're both empty," Jay said out loud.

Which didn't make sense.

Not if there was a piece of heavy wood inside the red one.

Jay squinted, looked at the red container and then said out loud, "But then . . . who said the piece had to be made of the same material as the other pieces?"

And suddenly, it made sense.

The piece was made of Styrofoam or some other light material to make you *think* that the red container was empty when really it wasn't.

The only reason that the blue container was there was so that by opening it, you would think that both containers were empty.

He didn't really think that the test was fair, since the blue container was only there to be a red herring and lead you down a wrong path . . . but he set about getting the red container open anyway.

He wondered why they didn't make the red container the red herring.

Then he stopped wondering about *anything*—other than getting the red container open.

It felt good to only have one thing to think about.

He tried twisting it, prying at the gap with his fingernail, biting on it with his teeth, banging it on the table . . . and a bunch of other things that all produced the same result:

A tightly sealed red container.

Now he was even more frustrated than before, because now he had the solution but he couldn't get the stupid container open to prove it.

In a fit of anger he threw the red container against the wall.

It didn't open.

He picked up the instructions and read them.

"After you have finished with the puzzle, proceed through the door on your left. If you do not wish to continue with the testing, proceed through the door to your right."

Now, the *instructions* didn't even make sense.

They didn't say he had to put the puzzle together; they said, "When you are finished with the puzzle . . ."

Maybe *that* was it.
Jay thought about the words.

Maybe he didn't have to *finish* the puzzle; he just had to be finished *with it*.

It made sense.

But then it didn't make sense.

Why would the people giving the test, give a test in which the correct answer was *no answer*?

He walked over to where the red container had landed and picked it up.

Now it was dented.

"How much more grievous are the consequences of anger than the causes of it," he said out loud. It was a quote by Marcus Aurelius he remembered from high school. Sometimes he thought it was the *only* thing he remembered from high school.

He went back and sat down at the table.

Then he picked up the blue container and pulled the lid off easily. He examined it as close as he could while he took it on and off.

It was effortless.

He put the container next to its lid back on the table.

He picked up the red container and pulled on the lid.

Nothing.

No movement whatsoever.

He picked up the blue container again and, seeing that the lid was still on the table, reached for the lid too. When he did, his finger slipped inside the container and he felt something.

Not much, but something.

He rubbed his finger inside the blue container then examined it.

There on the end of his finger was some sort of lubricant.

He rubbed his finger and thumb together and marveled at how effortlessly the two could move without friction.

He rubbed his finger in the bottom of the blue container and looked again.

Sure enough, there was some sort of clear lubricant in the bottom of the container, so thin that it was virtually invisible.

He looked inside the lid of the blue container and ran a clean finger around the rim.

A close examination showed that the lubricant was there too.

With fast movements, he picked up the red container and scraped some of the lubricant off his finger into the gap between the lid and the container.

With a slight nod to heaven, he pulled on the lid.

It moved.

Not much, but some.

It was enough to convince Jay that he was on the right path.

He rubbed his finger inside the blue container and gingerly tried to get as much of the lubricant into the growing gap on the red container as he could.

He pulled again.

More movement.

He went through the process again.

And again.

Until finally . . .

the lid came off.

Looking inside the now open red container Jay said out loud . . .

"That doesn't make any sense."

It was empty.

He sat down at the table and looked at the puzzle with the piece missing, then at the two containers.

He looked at the instructions.

He had two choices.

The door to the right, or the door to the left.

Quit, or continue.

He was physically tired, mentally exhausted and completely lacking in motivation.

He had done his best, but it didn't appear his best was good enough.

There was a piece of the puzzle missing—and he didn't know where to find it.

What if he opened the door to the left and tried to continue, only to find someone standing there asking for the puzzle piece?

What if that person then showed him where the piece was?

He would feel the same way he did when he gave up on one of those mixed-up letter games when GNOEHU could be scrambled to spell ENOUGH but he couldn't see it until he turned the newspaper upside-down and read it in the answers.

Only now it wasn't a stupid game; it was his life he was playing with.

He needed to think more.

But he was tired of thinking.

Why couldn't the last piece have been in the red container? Why couldn't the piece have fit perfectly and little streams of confetti fallen from the ceiling while a band played some song that made him feel good for finishing?

Now *that* would have made sense.

But it didn't happen that way.

And it didn't make sense.

What *did* make sense was that he failed.

The last piece was still to be found
        and he couldn't find it.

And if he was truthful, he didn't care anymore. All he wanted now was to go home.

"Screw this," he said out loud as he got up and walked to the door on his right.

But when his hand hit the doorknob, it dawned on him.

There's no disgrace in failing.
But quitting . . . Where's the honor in that?

When he opened the door to his left, no one was waiting for him with their hand out looking for the missing puzzle piece.

It was just a room with a table in the middle of it that contained a clock, a note . . .

and the missing piece of the puzzle.

On the note was a message in the familiar type.

"You have 20 seconds to finish the puzzle."

The clock beeped and started counting down as a soft voice counted along with it, "20 . . . 19 . . . 18 . . ."

Jay calmly picked up the missing piece and with a smile on his face, went back into the previous room and picked up the odd-shaped piece (that now wasn't so odd with all of the other pieces in it).

Jay turned the whole puzzle over until he could see the spot where the missing piece went.

"15 . . . 14 . . . 13 . . .," the clock droned from the other room.

With a shake of his head he inserted the piece into the hole that was shaped just like it.

"10 . . . 9 . . ."

It didn't fit.

"8 . . . 7 . . ."

It sort of fit, but it sort of didn't fit too.

"6 . . . 5 . . ."

It was the right shape and the right size, but it didn't slide in and lock into place like the other pieces.

"4 . . . 3 . . ."

And right then, *without thinking*, Jay placed a little bit of the lubricant from the blue container on the missing piece and it slid into place and locked.

The clock stopped.

Jay stood there in the silence and examined the now completed puzzle. He reveled in the simple fact that now, with all the pieces perfectly fit together, it made sense.

Then it dawned on him. The only reason he knew about the lubricant was because he'd kept trying to find the missing piece in the previous room.

And right then, when he finished thinking that thought, a band started playing and confetti dropped from the ceiling . . .

because Jay wasn't
  three-quarters of the way
    through the test . . .

he was at the end.

You don't have to possess all of the answers, right now.

Or, to say it positively . . .

Sometimes the missing piece in the puzzle of life
can only be found by moving ahead
without it.

SIX | give in to the positive

"Success isn't permanent, and failure isn't fatal."
—Mike Ditka

As the couple looked off into the seemingly unending sea, they tried to imagine living in paradise.

As long as they looked down the cliff toward the beach with its crashing surf and lush green foliage, it was easy. However, if they turned and looked at the dilapidated house with its piles of trash and dirty walls . . . it wasn't easy.

It wasn't impossible, just not easy.

The reason it wasn't impossible was because the man made houses for a living and he knew exactly what it would take to turn this makeshift landfill into paradise.

The reason it wasn't easy was because he didn't speak the area's language and didn't know the local tradesmen like he did where he lived.

But, when everything had been weighed in, they decided to take on the two-year project.

"Oh, one last question," they said. "Do you get hurricanes here?"

Which seemed like a reasonable question, since they were going to pour years of work and thousands of dollars into this house along the beach.

Here was the reply: "The last time a hurricane hit here was 80 years ago, and even then, it wasn't a very big one."

With a sigh of relief, they signed the papers.

Now let us break from the story to ask a question:

Should that reply have given the couple consolation or concern?

Let's think of the world as being divided up among the following types of people:

Extreme Optimists (always optimistic)
Optimistic Realists (more optimist than pessimist)
Pessimistic Realists (more pessimist than optimist)
                              and . . .
Extreme Pessimists (These people prefer to be called Extreme Realists, but in my experience, they find the worst possible outcome and camp there. That makes them extreme pessimists to me.)

Next, let's evaluate the likely reaction about the hurricane response, as it would come from each of these views.
                    An *Extreme Optimist* might say:
"A hurricane will not hit here in my lifetime."

An *Optimistic Realist* might say:

"Hurricanes here are so rare, and so small, that they are of no concern."

A *Pessimistic Realist* might say:

"Hurricanes have hit here in the past, which means they probably will do so in the future."

And an *Extreme Pessimist* might say:

"If there hasn't been a hurricane to hit here in 80 years, this place is due for one."

A big one.

Granted, there are more variations than just these four, but for the sake of this story, we will say that most of the people in the world will fit into these categories rather nicely.

So, back to the story . . .

Within days of signing the papers, the house was hit with a class five hurricane (the most dangerous class).

End of story.

Well, almost the end of the story.

Because, before we end the story, we first need to ask the Big Question:

How can you justify being a positive person when extremely negative people are right a lot of the time?

Let's consider the following observations:

Being a positive person means accepting *all* of the options above as being valid.

Being a positive person is *not* choosing one viewpoint and saying it will happen; it is saying that no matter which one of them happens, you will make the best of it.

Most importantly, being a positive person means *not* worrying about a future outcome, because even if the most extreme negative outcome happens, it will have a positive benefit at some point in the future. (Remember, the game is longer than you think. And even if you cannot imagine it, there's a raft around the corner.)

Finally, being a positive person is not about external circumstances; it is about the internal response to those circumstances.

And you control your internal response.

Don't you?

Postscript: The house survived the hurricane with only a few roof tiles lost. In fact, the hurricane blew away piles of trash and knocked down a dilapidated wall, which actually increased the value of the property.

Don't give in to the negative.

Or, to say it positively . . .

Positive results can happen from negative events.

SEVEN | soaked with sadness

"The truth is that there is nothing noble in
being superior to somebody else. The only real nobility is
in being superior to your former self."
—Whitney Young

What was once my protection from the elements
       is now my enemy.

What was once my hope for the future is now the thing that could take my future away.

Like water seeping into the clothes of a drowning man, sadness has seeped over my soul until I am soaked, my ability to fight overpowered.

Looking for something or someone to save me, I find none.

Looking inside my soul for the will to save myself, I find none.

As I sink deeper into the darkness, the light above grows distant and dim.

As I sink deeper into the darkness, my hope for rescue grows distant and dim.

The thought of giving in to the darkness is a comfort.
My soul is tired of fighting.

The life-giving air that used to come effortlessly with a slight rise of my breast is now only possible with enough strength to raise the sea . . .

and I have no strength.

Images of my family seem to appear in the bubbles fleeing to the surface. Images of my hopes and dreams appear too.

I give a feeble kick to see them more, but in an instant they are gone.

I sink deeper into the cold darkness.

The end is near.

My body continues to float downward, but I am now outside of it.

I study myself.

I was well prepared for this trip.

Thoroughly protected from any outside element, I had covered myself with the best garments possible. If things had stayed as they were, I would have thrived. But now, in the environment I find myself, I am totally vulnerable.

In the beginning it was only a slight miscalculation, a mistake that appeared to be fully correctable.

It was the correction that caused the calamity.

Or was it the correction of the correction?

The story comes to mind of two ocean liners. The ships' captains made adjustments in their courses to avoid a collision . . . only to cause the collision through their adjustments.

It was a comedy of errors.

Without the comedy.

Their passengers must have surely found themselves in as cold of a darkness as I now do.

I look at my attire and marvel at how something that was so valuable just a short time ago is now worthless.

If only a giant hook would come down from the surface and bring me back to where I had been.

True, I would be a far distance from where I wanted to be, but I would at least have enough knowledge to avoid this failure.

It would be wonderful.

I embarrass myself by looking for a hook.

Of course, there is none.

Granted, should a hook *have* appeared, it would have been a miracle . . .

but I am convinced that only a miracle can save me now.

The embarrassment fades.

                I don't care anymore.

Then an idea strikes me with the force of an electric shock.

I realize that I am not sinking.

It is the attire I put on for protection that is sinking and taking me down with it.

The protector is now the destroyer.

I start ridding myself of its heaviness as I think about floating back to the surface.

I imagine being able to fill my lungs with the sweet air of freedom.

Then I imagine the elements as they were when I fell into this hole, and realize that without my protection I would be defenseless.

The elements would certainly have their way with me as the deep does now.

I am doomed above and below.

So I stop all effort.

The dark gets darker and the cold colder.
There is no hope.

Up above, at the spot I where I fell,
a man waits and watches.

Even though I never saw him, he saw me. He watched me fall but was too late to catch me, and too weak to save me.

He now waits by the hole with a blanket
and a tin of hot drink.

He is not a miracle. He is just a man.

But he's enough of a miracle to save me.

He is as real as you or me.

But because I didn't see him,
he doesn't exist in my mind.
And because he doesn't exist in my mind,
he cannot help me . . .

because I gave up.

Don't limit yourself to what you can see.

Or, to say it positively . . .

Believe in the unseen.

EIGHT | a raft in the city

"Being defeated is often a temporary condition. Giving up
is what makes it permanent."

—Marilyn vos Savant

With one ring of the phone, the young woman's face
lit up with hope and anticipation.

This was the call she had worked and sacrificed for years to
receive.

Her dedication was limitless.
Her understanding profound.
Her passion immense.
Her intelligence unquestioned.
Her recommendations stellar.

Finally, she would have her own classroom.

Pleasantries were exchanged, then the news.

Her face conveyed the news to those of us across the table from her.

It wasn't good.

With a slight shake of her head, the news was confirmed.

Hope was gone.

The others watched and tried to hide their disappointment as she listened in stunned silence for the reason.
It wasn't her dedication.
It wasn't her understanding.
It wasn't her passion.
It wasn't her intelligence.
And it certainly wasn't
        for lack of recommendations.

It was her lack of experience.

It was her only weakness.

She rubbed her head slightly, thanked the caller for the consideration and hung up the phone.
Quietly, she relayed the details.

Very un-quietly, the others proclaimed the event a travesty.

"They knew how much experience you had after your first interview!"

"They just stole six weeks of your time!"

She didn't really hear them.
She was too frightened.
This was her second rejection.

Time was running out.
All the good jobs had been taken.
Classes would soon begin.

Without her.

The thought of going back to waiting tables crossed her mind.
She became angry with herself.
She had turned down the first job she was offered in order to be available for a school that eventually turned her down.

She fully grasped the irony.

Taking the disappointment in stride, she managed to find enough energy to start searching again.

Now, after a month and a half of interviews, she was back where she started.

No . . . after a month and a half of interviews, she was *further back* than where she started, because now there was less time.

The thought of waiting tables again crossed her mind.
She became sad.
Wasn't it enough that she had excelled at her work?

Wasn't it enough that she had sacrificed friends and family to get the knowledge and the diploma?

Hadn't she paid enough of a price?

Wasn't the loneliness of the last year enough?

The thought of waiting tables again crossed her mind.

She became afraid.

She wanted her own classroom.

The others did their best to encourage.

"This job wasn't meant to be."
"There are other schools."
"It's still possible."
"There is still time."

They had said the same things after the first rejection.

Would they say the same after the third?

The fourth?

The thought of waiting tables crossed her mind.
She needed sleep.

But sleep wouldn't come.
Regrets, fears and worries came effortlessly.

But sleep, hope and determination
        couldn't be found anywhere.

The others had to go on with their lives.

She had to go to Kinko's to make more copies of her resume and references.
There were only two openings left.

One of them offered her a job.

But not for her own classroom.

Oh, well. It was better than waiting tables.

All options had been explored.

This was the best she could hope for.

Actually, it wasn't.

There was a raft around the corner that she didn't know about.

In her favorite part of town, close to a beautiful apartment, there was a school.
A school that had been interviewing teachers for six months, looking for a teacher who had limitless dedication, profound understanding, immense passion, unquestioned intelligence and stellar recommendations.

After six months of interviews, they decided that the teacher they wanted couldn't be found.

They would have to make do.

Except there was a raft around the corner that *they* didn't know about.

All that was needed was for the school without a teacher and the teacher without a school to meet.

Except neither knew the other existed.

And they still wouldn't know each other existed to this day, if it weren't for a phone call.

A phone call to every school with a simple question:

"Do you have any openings
        for primary school teachers?"

Within seven days from the time of that phone call, the teacher found herself living in that beautiful apartment in her favorite part of town and teaching . . .

        in her own classroom.

Mental failure almost always precedes physical failure.

Or, to say it positively . . .

When you keep going, so do your options.

NINE  strike two

"Mentally, it's almost like you give up. You never want to say you give up, and you go back out there and give it everything you've got, but mentally, it's tough to get past this feeling you're defeated."

—Al Leiter
Commenting on losing the first three games in a seven game series.

He didn't know if it had ever been done,
    but he told the girls it had.

   "I've seen teams get *ten points* with two outs in the bottom of the ninth."

The Durango High School Girl's Fast Pitch Softball Team was behind by seven points and down to their last batter.

"Strike TWO!"

Correction. They were down to their last strike.

He motioned for the girl in the batter's box to come over closer to the dugout.

She looked at him, confused, and then focused on the pitcher. "CALL TIMEOUT!" the coach yelled at the batter.

The batter looked at the ump and said, "Timeout," and stepped out of the box.

Just then, a ball came flying into the catcher's glove.

The coach of the Durango High School Girl's Fast Pitch Softball Team was on his way to home plate in a flash.

"WE CALLED TIMEOUT!"

The umpire shook his head and walked toward the livid coach. "Coach, you know that I have to *grant* a timeout. She can't just step out of the box!"

"But I just did what you told me to do!" the batter whined, almost in tears.

The coach was now about two inches away from the umpire's face. "Well, you must have said something; otherwise she wouldn't have stepped out!"

"If you want to be here for the end of this game, you'd better watch what you say," the ump said, looking the coach straight in the eye.

The coach thought about what he just heard.

The ump turned to the opposing team's dugout and yelled, "Ball ONE!"

With that, the opposing team's coach headed to the plate for his own heated discussion with the umpire.

Seeing his chance, the Durango girl's softball team coach turned the batter so that she could only see his face.

"I want you to only think of one thing when you go back out to the plate," he said sternly.

"What's that, coach?" she asked.

"Think about the last time you got a hit off of this pitcher."

"But I've never gotten a hit off this pitcher."

"OK, then I want you to think of one other thing."

She nodded, and then waited for the one other thing.

He tried to think of what the other thing was.

"PLAY BALL!" the umpire yelled.

The coach looked over at the umpire then looked back at the batter.

"Is this pitcher the best pitcher in our league?"

"No."

"Have you ever gotten a hit off of a better pitcher?"

"Yes."

"Then you're a better hitter than she is a pitcher."

"COACH!" the umpire had lost all patience.

"Think about *that!*" the coach said as he turned her toward the plate, half expecting her to ask a follow-up question.

But she didn't.

She went up to the plate and thought about only that thing.

"YOU'RE A BETTER HITTER THAN SHE IS A PITCH-ER!" he yelled toward the plate.

And that was exactly what she was thinking about.

In fact, she was still thinking about that when the ball hit the catcher's glove.

"BALL TWO!"

Loud groans could be heard from the opposing team.

"Come on ump; let's get this game over with!" yelled the other team's coach.

"Then get your pitcher to throw strikes!" the ump yelled back.

He had had enough of both coaches.

The catcher tried to encourage the pitcher as she threw the ball back, "Just one more strike . . . that's all you need!"

So the pitcher tried just a little bit harder.

Which caused her to hold onto the ball just a little bit tighter . . . and throw just a little bit harder.

The ump had to duck down behind the catcher to keep from getting hit in the face with the catcher's glove.

"Ball three," the ump said as he popped his head up from behind the catcher, knowing there would be no argument from the opposing team.

The coach from the other team walked out to the mound and said, "She hasn't hit a pitch from you all season. Quit trying to nibble at the plate. Throw a strike down the middle of the plate."

Then he turned and walked back to the dugout.

"Coach?" came a slightly confused voice from the pitcher's mound. The coach spun around and with lasers for eyes and forcing the syllables through clenched teeth said, "WE DON'T HAVE ALL DAY TO WAIT FOR YOU TO THROW A STRIKE. DO IT NOW!

So she swallowed her question and threw a strike.

Only the coach never saw it.

That's because he wasn't off of the field when the ball left the pitcher's hand.
Which meant his back was to the mound.
And his feet were still on the field.
Which was against the rules.
The ump thought about calling a timeout, but he didn't really want to spend the next fifteen minutes explaining why.

When the catcher looked at the mound and saw the ball on the way to the plate, she had no idea what was headed her way. She hadn't given the pitcher a sign, and therefore didn't have a clue what kind of pitch was headed her way. Although, judging from the speed the ball was traveling and the path it was taking, it didn't take long for her to figure out that it was a fastball—and it was headed straight for the center of the plate.

It also didn't take the *batter* long to figure out what was headed her way either. Because of all the people who were surprised to see a ball hurtling toward home plate, the batter was not one of them.

You see . . . she was a fastball hitter.

And ever since the coach talked to her, the only thing she had been thinking about was the fact that deep down inside herself, she knew she could hit a fastball from any pitcher in the league.

Now she had a fastball headed straight toward her . . . and she was ready.

What happened next is in question.

What *isn't* in question is the fact that the pitcher threw a very hard fastball right down the middle of the plate.

Nor is there any question about whether the batter hit that very hard fastball that was headed right down the middle of the plate.

Because she hit it.
Actually, she smoked it.

Straight back to the pitcher.

But the pitcher didn't catch it.

The ball glanced off her shoulder and careened into the outfield. Everybody who was at the game says that she was lucky the ball didn't hit her in the head.

Her coach wasn't so lucky.

He *did* get hit in the head . . .
      with the *bat*.

Which is where all the questions come in.

The catcher says that the batter hit the ball and then threw the bat at the opposing team's coach.

The batter says that the catcher stuck her glove out too far over the plate, which caused her to hit the glove and thereby lose her grip on the bat.

The ump says he didn't see the bat hit the coach (although secretly he wished he did). He was watching the ball to see if the pitcher was going to catch it.

The coach of the Durango High School Girl's Fast Pitch Softball Team says that if the other team's coach hadn't been on the field, he wouldn't have been hit. And so it doesn't make any difference what caused the batter to lose her grip.

The opposing team's coach has no opinion.

Mainly because he can't remember *anything* . . .
      yet.

By the time the paramedics had hauled the coach off of the field, it was too dark to continue, so we *still* don't know who won the ballgame.

But we do know that the two coaches coached in very different ways.

The coach for the opposing team taught his girls to react to fear and intimidation and to look outside of themselves for motivation.

The coach for the Durango High School Girl's Fast Pitch Softball Team never gave up and taught his girls to look inside *themselves* for motivation.

External situations can change. If a person reacts to those eternal situations, they will forever be at their beck and call.

Internal motivation means that an individual is aware that even if they do their best, they may lose. But then, losing is part of life and this game is not THE game because there will always be other games in life.

So while we may not know who won this ballgame, we *do* know which team will win in the game of life.

Don't let outside circumstances
determine your internal motivation.

Or, to say it positively . . .

A positive response to a negative circumstance
produces a positive result.

Dedicated to the 2004 World Series Champions
The Boston Red Sox

(The first team to win a Championship series
after losing the first three games)

TEN | the first eight balls don't count

"The world is round and the place which may seem like
the end may also be only the beginning."
—Ivy Baker Priest, in *Parade*

In the billiard game of Nine-Ball, if you sink every ball on the
table, and your opponent only sinks the nine ball, you lose.

George hated Nine-Ball.

If he got the first eight balls in, the other player would put the
nine ball in the pocket and win the game.

If the other player got the first eight balls in and left the nine ball, George would be so terrified of losing that he would miss the shot.

If you asked him, George would say he was cursed.

A slight exaggeration, but that's the way he felt.

Even if you *didn't* ask him,
      George was a failure.

      Unfortunately, this is *not* an exaggeration.

Everything George tried, failed.

Actually . . .
George didn't even have to try anything to fail.

      George could fail *without* trying.

      As sad as that sounds, it's true.

So one day he decided to *try* to fail. His logic was that since he failed at everything, when he failed at failing he would actually be succeeding. (Now you can see why George didn't have any friends.)

Well, he failed.

It turns out that George was so good at failing that even when he tried to *fail* at failing; he failed, because failing was the only thing he succeeded at. (George loved to explain things like this at parties, which explains why he was no longer invited to parties.)

Then one day George read a book that said if you think optimistic thoughts, optimistic things would happen to you.

So he decided that from that moment on, he would live optimistically.

It failed.

The way George tells it, on the first day of his optimistic journey, he missed the bus, got caught in a rainstorm without his umbrella, ran out of cash at the lunch counter, spilled his coffee on his desk and got lost trying to find the drycleaner where he left his new suit.

The problem was that George didn't have anyone to tell this to. See, everyone knew that George only talked about the bad things that happened to him and so nobody wanted to talk to him.

George was a lonely man with no friends.

If there *had* been anybody for George to talk to, they would have told him that on any given day, thousands of people have missed the bus or missed an appointment because they got caught in the rain without an umbrella. And they would have said that those very same people had ended up short of cash for lunch so they only bought coffee—only to spill it on their desks.

OK, they probably couldn't say that a lot of people get lost trying to find their drycleaner—at least not with a straight face—but it's very likely that at some point in their lives, quite a few people have changed dry cleaners only to go to the old one to pick up their clothes . . . and that is pretty close to getting lost.

But the problem with George wasn't the fact that bad things happened to him; the problem with George was that George had a habit of leaving out any of the *good* things that happened to him.

Like the time when he was trying to find his drycleaner.

If he were telling the story, he would leave out the part about the girl reading a book in the park.

He asked her if she knew where the drycleaner was.

Now that was a good thing.

Not because she knew where the drycleaner was,

because she didn't.

But she *did* know the building where George lived, and by helping him find his way home, he actually remembered where his drycleaner was.

Although when he got to the drycleaner, he found out that he had already picked up his suit and it was at home hanging in his closet.

Now if you're thinking that George really *was* cursed . . . with a short memory, that couldn't be further from the truth.

George could remember very difficult names from insignificant historical events that happened a hundred years ago.

Which was good, since his job was doing historical analysis and research for a museum . . .

Which was bad, since that meant he spent most of his time in a small room doing research about people who had been dead for a century or two rather than talking with people who were alive and his own age . . .

Which was good, since people who were alive and his own age didn't *want* to talk to him because all he talked about were people who had been dead for a century or two *and* the fact that he was cursed . . .

All except the girl he met in the park.

She *loved* talking about people who had been dead for a century or two.

Which left no time for George to tell her that he was cursed.

But then, after he met her, he couldn't honestly say he was cursed anymore—because cursed people don't find true love.

Especially if they find true love . . .

    when they are really trying to find . . .

    a drycleaner.

It's not how you start;
it's how you finish.

Or, to say it positively . . .

Be thankful for happy accidents.

ELEVEN | you have to give up something to get something

> "If my hands are fully occupied in holding on to
> something, I can neither give nor receive."
> —Dorothee Solle

Mary didn't know that when you proclaimed a truth to be universal, the universe took notice.

So just one day after she proclaimed in her newspaper article, "It's a universal truth that you have to give up something to get something," she found herself on trial before the Universal Court.

Now, most humans don't know about the Universal Court because very few are ever invited there. The reason very few are ever invited there is because in the whole universe, it seems that the human race is just not very well liked. It's not really fair, because humans really are not that much more distasteful as a group than the Gorgites or Ziiutions, but stereotypes have a way of staying around long after they have been proven wrong.

In The Universal Court, humans are only summoned at night after they have gone to sleep. The reason for this unusual timing is that the court has found that when humans awake the following day, they are more than likely to assume that the whole affair was nothing more than a curious dream.

The particular court that would hold Mary's trial was the Second Court of Universal Truth. It was in session on a small planet in the middle of a globular cluster in the constellation Canes Venatici.

Dressed in the worn flannel pajamas she had slept in since college, Mary was announced simply as Defendant 3iG997 and ushered into the immense courtroom.

She would have no trouble believing that it was all a dream when she awoke the following morning.

The courtroom consisted of a series of seven concentric circles that rose from the floor to the ceiling, with each ring supporting the desks and chairs from which the members of the court appeared to work.

Actually, to Mary, the members appeared to be *not* working, since most were either asleep or talking amongst themselves about personal matters.

A very large creature with large eyes on both sides of a flat skull that resembled a hammerhead shark was seated at the head of the room under the flag of the Universe. With a thunderous voice he spoke to Mary directly.

"Defendant 3iG997, do you know why you are here?"

"No," was all that Mary could coax from her hesitant throat.

"You are here to defend your proposed universal truth," came the reply.

"My universal . . . what?"

In unison a gasp erupted from throughout the courtroom.

From the top circle closest to the ceiling, a high-pitched whiny voice yelled out, "I told you this proceeding was unnecessary. She doesn't even know what she said!"

May looked up toward the voice and saw a skinny rail of a creature that reminded her of Don Knotts from an old episode of *The Andy Griffith Show*.

Another strange looking thing, that could be best described as a mop with eyes, yelled from the other side of the room at the

Don Knotts-looking creature, "So what? You don't know what you're saying most of the time either!"

With that, the creatures on the left side of the room all cheered.

"Order, order!" yelled Hammerhead.

"We should have tried her in absentia, like we did 3 earth orbits ago!" continued the Don Knotts character.

Unknown to Mary, three years before, she had made another statement that had required the attention of the Second Universal Court of Truth. During a particularly dark period of time in her own life, she had written: "It's a universal truth that the hardest time to maintain a positive attitude is when you need it the most."

Her article never went into detail about what it was that drew her to this conclusion, but instead simply commented that she never felt more stupid than when she chose to believe that it was *possible* for a positive outcome to come out of a negative situation.

That feeling of stupidity was increased the next day when she received hundreds of letters and e-mails, which asked her to prove how anything positive came out of the Holocaust, September 11th or, as one mother asked in a tear-stained letter, a child being abducted.

As she sat and stared at the letters that included so many comments of hate and sadness, she could only agree that there were horrible things happening in the world and it was indeed very difficult to imagine a positive outcome from even her own personal situation, let alone the myriad of catastrophes recounted in the letters.

She then wrote a follow-up article where she tried to defend herself against the statements made by her critics rather than defend her original comment (a common mistake made in almost every debate). The article stated that without the knowledge of *every* outcome of *every* person who had been touched by the trage- dies, it was impossible to declare that *nothing* good had transpired from them. That comment only inflamed the readers even more. The result was that the next day, she found herself on a morning news show answering charges from a Senator who maintained she had written that the Holocaust was a good thing.

By that time, the comment had taken on a life of its own and she regretted ever making it.

She might have changed her mind if she had known, that after two days of deliberation, the Universal Court agreed with her and voted unanimously that indeed, it is a universal truth that the hardest time to maintain a positive attitude is when you need it the most.

Back on the small planet in the middle of a globular cluster in the constellation Canes Venatici, the Hammerhead's gavel came down with such force that the room immediately quieted.

"Is there an Advocate?" Hammerhead asked, as he surveyed the members of the court.

There was a quiet murmur from the members of the court as they determined among themselves whether any of them wanted to defend Mary and her newest universal truth.

"Aye," came a quiet response from the front row, immediately followed by a very unquiet murmur from the rest of the chamber.

Mary strained to see whom it was who had spoken up. When she saw who it was, she couldn't help but sigh with deep disappointment. Her Advocate appeared to be a lump of pink jelly the size of a piano.

The rest of the room did not seem to share her feelings at all, since there seemed to be quite a stir about her defender. The bailiff standing next to Mary leaned close to her and said that her Advocate was none other than Oot, Chancellor of Dupio.

Now, to you and me, Oot the Chancellor of Dupio means nothing. But in the Second Universal Court, Oot was a legend. He rarely spoke up in court and took so few cases as an Advocate that when he did, it was an event.

"Dress the defendant," ordered Hammerhead.

The floor under Mary immediately gave way and with the same sound that you hear when you use one of those tubes at the bank drive-thru, Mary was swooshed to the defendant's table.

Once there, Mary was surprised to see that she was no longer wearing her flannel pajamas from college, but instead, a black gown of what appeared to be exceptionally fine silk. As she marveled at the gown, Oot spoke to her in a voice that was as smooth as the silk in her gown. "Only my defendants get gowns from Dupio. It's made from the finest material in the universe."

When Mary looked up from the magnificent gown to say thank you to her advocate, the words froze in her throat. The sight of her advocate was like nothing she had ever seen before.

The features of his face moved freely on the surface of his jelly-like skin. He was too immense to turn the whole of his body, so when he spoke to someone, only his face moved. Mary stared in awe as Oot carried on a conversation with the others around him. As one or another would seek his attention, his body would remain stationary, while his eyes, nose and mouth would travel in the general direction of the one talking to him.

The pink mound, the sight of which was disappointing from the edge of the courtroom, was magnificent when observed at close range. It appeared to have an inner light, which caused all around it to be bathed in a soft, warm glow.

After the initial shock, Mary was calmed.

Looking back down at the fine gown she was wearing, she made a mental note to try to write all of this down once she awakened.

Hammerhead dropped his gavel and announced: "The Second Court of Universal Law will now hear case FJ5-102995 with the distinguished representative from the region of Dupio as Advocate."

With that, the entire assembly raised their right hand (or whatever appendage they happened to have on the right side of their body) only to bring it down noisily to the top of their desks, followed by a loud grunt as each pounded their closed fist into the left side of their chest. As the sound from the desk banging and chest thumping reverberated through the chamber, each member nodded toward the direction of Oot.

With one more sound of his gavel, Hammerhead gave a nod toward Oot and the procession began.

The face of Oot turned toward the assembly and he began his remarks in a soft, silky voice that matched the magnificent smoothness of Mary's robe.

"For a universal law to be true, it must be true in every language, every culture and in every situation in every galaxy. This requirement is so stringent, that in the entire history of the Second Court of Universal Law, only a handful of laws have actually been found to be universal." His face turned and focused on

Mary. "As such, it is a great pleasure of mine to represent one of the recipients of a previous award."

Once again the entire assembly went through the gyrations of their right-hand salute, only this time they nodded toward Mary at its conclusion.

Oot continued, "It is my belief that the statement 'You must give up something to get something' is truly universal in scope and in application."

The squeaky voice of the Don Knotts character shattered the peacefulness of Oot's address like a piece of broken glass, "And I believe it is NOT."

Hammerhead dropped his gavel and gave an icy stare toward the top of the assembly where Don sat.

"The members will refrain from comments until the Advocate has finished his initial defense!"

"There is no defense!" whined Don. "This case is so unfounded it shouldn't even be heard."

Hammerhead slammed his gavel down and raised his voice to match. "Bailiff! Remove the representative from . . ."

The calm voice of Oot interrupted him. "No, let him speak. I grant him free discussion."

Hammerhead gritted his teeth and said in a low voice, "Free discussion has been requested and granted . . . as long as it is CIVIL."

Don stood up and addressed the assembly. "I regret that my behavior has offended the speaker, but I must assert that I came up with ten instances that eliminate this proposed law from consideration without even thinking about it."

The mop with eyes shouted out, "What's new? You never think about *anything*."

Hammerhead slammed the gavel once again and shouted, "Only one representative at a time is granted free discussion. All others, please refrain comment until recognized."

"List your ten," uttered Oot in his calm voice.

"There is no need for ten, for the first will be all that is needed to stop this silly discussion."

"Do you relinquish your right to present the other nine?" asked Hammerhead.

"No, I shall hold them in reserve, although I cannot see how they shall be needed."

"Then proceed," ordered Hammerhead.

Don took a deep breath. Then, in a magnanimous gesture waved toward Mary, he said, "I request first that the defendant give us a summary example."

Everyone in the chamber looked at Mary in unison.

Mary first looked at the skinny man with his hand stretched toward her, and then she looked at the glowing mass of pink next to her.

She tried to speak but nothing emerged from her throat.

Seeing her dilemma, Oot spun his face around and spoke to an assistant nearby. Immediately the assistant poured a glass of water and handed it to Mary.

While she sipped the water, Oot spoke to the assembly.

"May I speak for the defendant?"

"Feel free," answered Hammerhead.

Oot spoke in a warm, soft voice. "It is obvious to me that we must give up the shape of the wood to receive the heat of the fire . . . and we must give up the pleasure of a fruit to receive the nutrients inside."

Mary coughed on a sip of water and Oot looked at her quickly to see if she was OK. She nodded at him and he continued, "Unlike my esteemed colleague, I cannot think of a single example that refutes the statement that we must give up something to get something."

Don could take it no more.

"A thief!"

Shocked by his outburst, the assembly turned and looked at Don. Enjoying the attention, he stood silently, waiting for Mary to take the bait.

Oot looked at Mary but the only thing she could muster was another weak cough.

Rather than ask Mary to speak, Oot asked Don to clarify his remarks. "What about a thief?"

Don answered with a slight smirk in his voice "By definition, a thief is one who takes without paying. He *gets* something and *gives up* nothing."

"He gives up his honor!" shouted Mary with a surprisingly strong voice.

Don smiled. She had taken the bait. "A thief loses his honor *only* if he is caught—and then only if he is caught stealing too little."

A wave of laughter rippled through the court.

Don continued, "Every thief does *not* give up his honor. Some of the most honored men in history were at one time or another . . . thieves."

"But equally erroneous is the idea that a wealthy thief who is smart enough to remain at large gives up nothing for his craft," came Mary's quick reply.

Don jumped in with: "I must plead a certain ignorance on the subject of thievery. Perhaps we could consult with those on the opposite side of the aisle for clarification." With that, he ever so slightly pointed his finger in the general direction of the mop with eyes.

The room erupted into mixture of bedlam and laughter, depending on which side of the aisle the representative sat.

It took several large whacks of the gavel for Hammerhead to gain a modicum of order. When the room finally quieted, he stared at the Don Knotts character and said in a stern voice, "Insults will not be tolerated."

"My apologies," replied Don with feigned sincerity.

Mary cleared her throat and began again. "Every illegal activity requires a toll from its perpetrator. If not in guilt or fear, the simple loss of the thief's ability to discuss one's occupation publicly is something he must give up forever."

"The loss of open discussion on a career can hardly be considered giving up something."

Mary countered, "Regardless of your perception of the *value* of this loss of freedom, it is something that every thief must *give up* or they will most likely be *giving up* a far more valuable commodity . . . Namely, their *freedom*."

A low murmur ran through the courtroom as Don considered his response.

When he realized that he couldn't win with a thief as a protagonist, he decided to take a more moral tone.

"Then let us discuss what one is required to give up in order to get unconditional love."

The mop with eyes stood up and shouted out, "If he knew nothing of thievery, he knows less about *love*!"

The mop's side of the aisle erupted into howls of laughter. It was so loud that Mary could hardly hear the slamming of the Hammerhead's gavel.

"On the next outburst, I will request the bailiff to immediately remove any unrecognized speaker!" yelled the Hammerhead.

With a few titters still being heard, the room quieted.

The Don Knotts character picked up where he left off.

"Surely we all agree that, albeit rare, unconditional love *does* exist and as such requires nothing in return."

Mary had used the time it took for the uproar to settle down to think through her response, so she was ready for him. "Are you suggesting that it is possible for a woman to be walking down the street and suddenly and unexpectedly be granted unconditional love by a man who knows nothing of her and has received no encouragement from her whatsoever?"

Giggles started to be heard from the room but were immediately stopped cold by the stare of Hammerhead.

"While I have never personally seen it happen [more titters and coughs, followed by a disgusted look by Don], we cannot rule definitively that the incident is impossible. So, yes, let's use that scenario as a basis," replied Don.

Mary thought for a moment and then asked, "Does the woman radiate beauty?"

"No. Unlike you, she is not excessively beautiful to the point that she radiates beauty. Nor, like certain other creatures I have seen in the universe," he thought about casting a glance toward the mop but decided against it, "is she so excessively hideous that she warrants pity."

"Does she exude confidence?"

"No, nor does she appear helpless."

"Does she have a fetching smile?"

"No, she is toothless!" Don said with an exasperated tone.

"Is *he* a dentist?"

Loud laughter erupted—this time, even from Hammerhead.

When she could be heard, Mary spoke as if she were a defense attorney speaking to the jury. "You have stated that a man can give unconditional love with no encouragement from a woman, but that is a trap to divert our attention from the true subject we are discussing. Our discussion is not whether one can give something without getting something; it is exactly the opposite: You must *give up* something to *get* something.

"For this woman to receive this man's unconditional love she must acknowledge it. If she acknowledges it, she will expend some energy in doing so and that energy is at a cost to her. Therefore, she cannot receive his unconditional love without it costing her *some* amount of time and energy, both of which are very valuable commodities."

Don looked at Mary and then, shaking his head, looked at his notes.

After reading down the page, he saw something in his notebook that caught his eye. "This morning I received in the mail a coupon for a free lunch." He held up the coupon for all to see.

"There is no fine print, save the small comment that no other purchase is necessary. Therefore, the lunch is completely free with no strings attached; I am required to give up nothing to get something."

Don looked at Mary smugly.

Mary looked around the room as she said quietly, "Won't you be required to give up the coupon itself?"

Don stammered as he spoke "Well, that's not the point. The food is free, without obligation."

Mary knew she had him on this one but tried not to gloat. "Actually, the coupon *is* the point and you will be most certainly required to give up the coupon to get your free lunch."

Don shook his head as he realized he was losing to a technicality.

With his frustration evident, he shot examples out in rapid fire: "A conversation with a friend is without cost."
"On the contrary, it costs time," said Mary.

"A birthday present, dropped off anonymously at the door of a house, requires nothing in exchange."

"Your example takes place in the middle of the exchange, not the beginning, for surely there was time, or affection given to warrant a gift," she replied.

"It's from a stranger whose sole purpose in life is to give gifts to people he doesn't know!" shouted Don.

"Is it possible for you to give him *my* address?" asked Mary.

Loud laughter erupted again—this time even from Don Knotts.

Mary continued, "While I will agree that a gift left on the doorstep by a stranger appears at first glance to require nothing on the part of the receiver to get it, that is only true if the recipient does not actually *go to get it* off the doorstep."

Don recognized where she was going and stopped laughing.

"As in the case of the unconditional love example you previously mentioned, the moment one gives of their *time* to go get the gift and gives of their *energy* to lift it and open it, they have indeed given something to get it," finished Mary with the one-two punch of a prizefighter.

Oot smiled at Mary with approval.

Don stared at his list.

When it did not appear that he was going to continue, the Hammerhead asked quietly, "Representative, do you acquiesce?"

Don ignored the comment and studied his notes.

After reading through and discarding most of the items on his list he finally said, "A homeless man who never paid taxes and never spoke to anyone collapses on the sidewalk. Unknown to him, while he is in a comatose state, he is given an intravenous injection that saves his life . . ."

He then looked up with the look of man who has just put a king in checkmate with nothing more than a pawn.

"He has received *something* and given up *nothing*."

The courtroom went silent. It was if they had just watched a prizefighter who was falling to the canvas manage enough strength to land a roundhouse to the jaw of his opponent.

The entire chamber looked at Mary in shock. Mary looked at Oot and saw nothing but confidence in his floating face.

He leaned over to Mary and whispered, "You've got him right where you want him."

Mary waited for a bit more of an explanation but Oot wasn't saying anything more.

As the time passed, the Hammerhead asked Mary quietly, "Do you acquiesce?"

Don Knotts started receiving congratulatory handshakes from his colleagues in the upper levels of the courtroom.

With nothing coming from Mary's mouth, the Hammerhead lifted his gavel to declare that it was NOT a universal truth that you had to give up something to get something.

But before he could drop the gavel Mary spoke up firmly.

"He gave up control of his own body . . ."

Don stopped shaking hands and asked those around him what she had said.

Mary repeated herself, only louder, "He gave up control of his own body and in so doing, received medical care."

"That's ludicrous!" Don yelled from the top of the room.

"Is it?" Mary asked rhetorically. "As a sick man, he could have marched into any hospital and received care."
"He didn't know he was sick!" came Don's angry reply.

"So you are saying that a man who needed healthcare only received it after he lapsed into unconsciousness?"
Don had a pretty good idea that no matter how he answered the question he was going to regret it.
"Yes; sure!" he finally blurted out.

Mary smiled. Checkmate.

"So, while he was in control of his body, he *didn't* receive care. But when he gave up control of his body, he received it?"

Don tried to think of an answer but couldn't.

The Hammerhead's gavel came down loudly. "Decided! Be it hereafter known as a universal truth that one must give up something to get something!"
The entire assembly then gave Mary the loud salute along with a standing ovation.
She looked at Oot and caught a small wink from one of his floating eyes.

Then came the same "whooshing" sound she had heard before. And in a blink of an eye, Mary found herself sitting up in her own bed wearing her old college flannel pajamas, shivering in a cold sweat.

There was no question that it had all been a dream. The question was: Why had she dreamed it?

With no answer to be found in her room, she got up and made herself a cup of herbal tea and wandered around her house in the dark.

She finally sat down at her kitchen table, and with the steam from the tea comforting what had become a nagging headache, she tried in earnest to come up with a reason for the dream.

Nothing came to mind.

Two days later, while she stared at a black dress in a shop window, it hit her.

She needed to let go.

Her job was killing her.

Her newspaper was dying, her health was fading and her boss was an angry little man who resembled Don Knotts.

Twice during the last year she had turned down offers from new sources of media that would have brought more exposure for her column, but each time she found some way to classify them as "too risky."

Now as she thought back on her life, in every case that she could remember, wonderful things had happened when she "let go" of something that she was holding onto tightly. From the thrill of the backyard swing when she let go of her father, to the excitement of seeing her name in print when she "let go" of her sales job at the paper . . . Whenever she let go, Mary was able to take hold of something else that turned out to be much better.

Just then, a sales clerk came out of the store and startled her by asking, "Would you like to try the black dress on?"

Mary smiled and shook her head, "No, thanks."

"Then at least come in and feel the material," the pleasant but persistent clerk said as she opened the door for Mary to come in. "It's made from Dupioni silk . . . and it has to be the finest material in the universe!"

Negatives are easy to hold on to.

Or, to say it positively . . .

Let go . . . and go!

TWELVE | can fear change the weather?

"The only real prison is fear, and the only real freedom is freedom from fear."

—Aung San Suu Kyi

Chris is a real person.
  He is my friend.

Chris is insane.

  Not literally, just figuratively.

He skis down avalanche chutes.

  At night.

He climbs rock walls.

  Not the ones you see in gyms
      or on a cruise ship.
Chris climbs walls
    that are hundreds of feet high,
      where the only way to get up the wall is
        to wedge your fist in a crack and pull
            yourself up.

He has been at the helm of a sailing ship in the middle of a hurricane.

I know that sounds a bit far fetched, but I believe him.

He's my friend.

His father was a scientist who traveled the world and took Chris with him.

When other kids were in middle school drinking cokes and taking science classes, Chris was drinking beer and performing experiments in a remote part of the world.

Today, Chris is a consultant to the military on how to keep intruders out of the places where the government keeps its weapons that can destroy civilization with the push of a button.

Chris doesn't know where the button is, but he does know where the weapons are.

Which brings me to my point.

Chris does *not* live in fear.
    He *does* get afraid.

There is a difference.

If Chris lived in fear,
    he would never set foot on a rock again.

People die climbing rocks.

If Chris lived in fear, he would take a job that didn't have a button around that could destroy millions of people.
> The rest of us just
>> assume that there are horrible things
>>> being stored by our government . . .

Chris knows where they are.

But—and this is a very important "*but*"—

> if Chris were *never* afraid, he wouldn't be alive.

People really do die climbing rocks.

By recognizing fear, Chris is able to slow himself down to make
sure he is safe.

Even if the climb takes longer than expected.
Even if he has an appointment
> he needs to get to.

> Chris is *never* in a hurry.

Every piece of gear he puts into a rock wall is backed up with
two other pieces.
Which means that if he falls, three pieces of gear will have to
fail before he could hurt himself.
The odds of three pieces of gear failing are slim.
Unless they aren't put into the rock correctly.
Then they can all pop out of the rock, one right after the other.

Rock climbers call that a "zipper."

Chris has a saying, "Friends don't let friends zipper."

That's why Chris always takes time to put the gear in correctly.

That is also why he chooses his climbing partner very carefully.

You see, if his climbing partner fails, then all of the protective gear in the world won't protect him.

There's no backup for a climbing partner who fails.

If a climbing partner makes just one mistake at the wrong moment, he will probably see death.

Before every climb, Chris inspects his partner's gear and asks his partner to inspect his.

Then he asks this question: "Are you willing to trust your life to this gear?"

Then each climber asks the other: "Are you willing to trust your life to me?"

It's a solid reminder that rock climbing is a dangerous sport.

I am Chris's climbing partner.

Chris is not afraid that I will fail him.

That is probably why we are such good friends.

One day Chris was ice climbing a fourteen thousand- foot peak in Colorado.

It was a beautiful sunny day (as are most days in Colorado) and Chris was climbing with a *very* experienced climbing partner (not me).

The climb up to the top was perfect. The two of them had the right gear, the right clothing and the right experience to climb to the top.

On the way down,

the weather changed.

Quickly.

As it almost always does in Colorado.

And it didn't change for the better.

Suddenly the air was charged with so much electricity that Chris could hear static shocks jumping between the pieces of metal gear hanging from his climbing harness.

Then the wind started.

Then the snow started.

Then the visibility dropped to zero.

Which is not what you want visibility to do when you're climbing on ice at an elevation of fourteen thousand feet.

Chris knew of a spot that would offer them some protection until the weather cleared.

The problem was finding it.

The two of them inched their way over the mountain, but in the whiteout conditions it was not clear whether they were going up or down.

The clothing that was perfect for climbing in bright sunny weather now became paper-thin and offered little protection.

They stopped long enough to take out the additional clothing they had in their backpacks.

Like I said, they were experienced.

The clothing was enough to keep them from freezing to death until they could get to a place that was protected from the elements.

It was *not* enough to keep them from freezing to death if they *didn't* get to a place that was protected from the elements.

Finding that place was becoming more and more difficult . . .

because for all intents and purposes,

they were lost.

Not "lost" in the traditional sense of the word, because they knew which mountain they were on and, once the weather cleared, they knew how to get back down the mountain.

But *until* the weather cleared, they couldn't see where they had been or where they were going—which meant that they didn't know how to get from where they were, to where they needed to be.

Which is a pretty good description of being lost.

So Chris became afraid.

And like I said, it takes a lot for Chris to become afraid.

Only this time, he didn't just recognize danger; instead, his fear escalated to a point that Chris was very unfamiliar with.

He found himself hurrying.

When the hurrying caused mistakes,
the fear increased.

When the fear increased, so did the urge to hurry even more.

Chris's calm patience and ability to slow himself down was gone. In its place was a frantic pace and an ever-present fear that they wouldn't get out of the weather soon enough.

Then he stopped.

The mountain didn't stop him.
The ice didn't stop him.
The wind didn't stop him.
Exhaustion didn't stop him.

A thought stopped him.
And this was the thought:

"Can *fear* change the weather?"

His climbing partner yelled at him through the howling winds.

Chris couldn't hear him.

He could only hear his own voice as it spoke out loud to no one but himself.

"Can fear change the weather?"

Then once again, but louder . . .

"Can fear change the weather?"

He didn't have to answer the question.

He knew the answer.

The answer was "no."

Fear could *not* change the weather.
And with that thought, he slowed himself down.

And by slowing himself down, he was able to see things he couldn't have seen when he was hurrying.

Which meant he saw things that . . .
     told him where he was
     and where he needed to go.

So he went there.

Slowly.

    Safely.
        Surely.

                Without fear.

Because fear couldn't change the weather.

Fear is a flag to be recognized,
not a tent to be lived in.

Or, to say it positively . . .

Recognizing and overcoming fear produces profound peace,
even in the most fearful of situations.

THIRTEEN | life is a movie

"I like nonsense—it wakes up the brain cells. Fantasy is a necessary ingredient in living. It's a way of looking at life through the wrong end of a telescope . . . and that enables you to laugh at all of life's realities."

—Theodor S. Geisel

In a dark room with a scratchy, faded film being projected onto a dirty, off-white screen, Dean slumped in his chair.

Next to him, an ancient 16mm projector clattered away as it tugged on a roll of film.

Dean, along with the others in the class, had laughed when the machine was rolled in. It looked almost prehistoric. Even in

Dean's less-than-affluent high school, videotapes and televisions had replaced film projectors a decade prior.

Disregarding the ridicule, the teacher maintained that the information on this particular film reel had never been transferred to videotape. And with a flourish that was usually reserved for world premiers, he brought the machine to life.

Dean coughed into his hand to get his best friend Nick's attention. Nick and Dean had been friends since third grade, so they knew how to communicate with the least amount of effort possible. When Nick heard the cough, he acknowledged the signal by raising his eyebrows in an unspoken question mark. Dean nodded toward the teacher.

Nick looked toward the teacher and smirked. The image of the teacher was comical. With the light from the bright bulb of the projector reflecting off of his glasses, he studied the film intently as it unwound from the top reel, snaked through the machine and wound itself back onto the bottom reel.

Once he had safely followed a section of film all the way to the bottom, his eyes would repeat the loop and follow another section through the machine.

His concentration was so intense that it appeared to Dean that the film was not being moved by the noisy gears of the projector, but instead by the sheer force of the teacher's will.

Nick looked back at Dean and shook his head. With a large sigh, Nick placed his head on the top of the desk and closed his eyes in the hope of catching a few minutes of sleep.

Dean turned his attention back to the flickering image on the screen. As the camera panned across a sleepy town, he imagined a man in a lizard suit stomping on the little houses. When no lizard appeared, he too put his head on his desk and started to close his eyes.

But just before his eyes closed, he noticed something. He couldn't tell exactly what it was, but whatever it was, it caused him to sit up and look around the room in an effort to identify it.

He could see nothing interesting going on except the teacher studiously watching the projector.

And that wasn't very interesting.

He closed his eyes again.

"There," Dean said to himself as his eyes almost closed again.

There it was.

With his head on his desk, and with his eyes almost closed, he could see a single bright sliver of light as it highlighted a single frame of the film, just before it disappeared into the projector.

Opening his eyes wide open and sitting up in his chair, Dean noticed a small panel just above the lens with a significant dent in it. He smiled as he thought about some member of the student A/V club knocking the projector off its stand sometime in the distant past. It was a funny picture to him.

Which was more than he could say about the picture actually playing up on the screen.

He laid his head back down on his desk and watched as the light flickered on and off, exposing the single frame of film.

At 24 frames per second, an average movie contains 172,800 snapshots projected in front of your eyes. Your mind takes each of these 172,800 snapshots and then puts them together into one continuous story.

It's safe to say that not one of those 172,800 snapshots could tell the story as well, or as completely, as the sum total can.

A picture may be worth a thousand words, but a picture without any words usually creates more questions than answers.

Not even newspapers, where single pictures are the norm, run pictures without some text to provide the reader with the context of what is going on in the picture.

Dean looked back at the film on the screen and opened and shut his eyes quickly.

He kept opening and shutting his eyes as quickly as he could in an effort to freeze one frame of the film in his memory.

He heard a cough and thought that Nick was trying to get his attention . . .

Except the cough was coming from the direction of the projector.

Dean looked toward the projector and saw the teacher staring at him.

Apparently, the teacher had stopped watching the projector long enough to see Dean opening and shutting his eyes in rapid succession.

He didn't know what Dean was doing, but he knew that he wasn't paying attention to the film.

He gave Dean a scornful look and nodded toward the screen.

Dean shook his head in amazement. Nick was practically snoring on top of his desk and the teacher picked Dean to scold for not watching the film?!

When he turned his attention back to the film, he found that a monotonous voice was still droning on as the image faded from blue to beige, back to blue again.

Which was sort of interesting, since it was a black and white film.

Then, it happened.

The projector suddenly started making more noise than usual. The teacher's eyes darted around the projector in an effort to see if there was a problem.

There was.

With the voracious appetite of a school of piranhas, the projector started shredding the ancient film reel.

The horrified teacher yelped, and immediately switched the ON/OFF switch to the OFF position.

Nothing happened.

Well, that's not true. A lot happened.

The projector began spewing bits of film around the room at a rate of 24 frames per second.

Boys laughed and girls screamed as pieces of film with razor-like edges flew in their direction. The girls got a chance to laugh for themselves when Bobby Aaron, the starting quarterback on the football team, let out a high-pitched scream as a piece of celluloid sliced his nose.

In the middle of all of the screaming and confusion, Nick slept peacefully on his desk.

Also in the middle of all the screaming and confusion, the teacher was running out of buttons to push and switches to switch.

Seeing no other alternative and wanting to stop any more of his precious film from being destroyed, the teacher yanked on the long power cord that connected the projector with the wall outlet. Unfortunately, the cord was wrapped around Bobby Aaron's chair, and instead of unplugging the projector as he had intended, the teacher's yank violently upturned the normal student/chair relationship that Bobby (and the chair) had been enjoying up to that point.

Much to the enjoyment of Jeff Clair, the school chess champion (a frequent recipient of rude remarks from the football team), for the second time that day, Bobby Aaron let out a scream that matched the pitch and intensity of the most hysterical girl as he landed on the floor with his chair on top of him.

The teacher divided his mortified looks between the toppled Bobby and the projector that was devouring film non-stop.

"Unplug it! Unplug it!" The teacher yelled as he tried to pick Bobby off the floor. Of course no one did, since the film-eating projector had now become the high point of the day.

Maybe the year.

Oblivious to it all, bits of film were starting to build up on Nick like some kind of post-apocalyptic celluloid ash. Nick was the youngest of four brothers, and as such had been tormented by his older siblings during sleep for most of his life. At some point he had discovered that the best way to make it stop was by ignoring it.

Today (inside his sleeping head), he had convinced himself that all of the chaos and the noise around him was nothing more than his three brothers trying to get him to wake up. The last thing he was going to do was give them the satisfaction of doing so.

Dean sat back in his chair and watched it all with the appreciation of man who was seeing his prayers being answered. This was better than a man in a lizard suit stomping on the little village.

Way better.

Finally tiring of the noise and the mayhem, Mary Weston quietly leaned over and unplugged the cord from the wall that was near her desk. Mary was a quiet person who liked quiet things. She could have stopped the machine much earlier but the scene was far too entertaining to stop, even for a quiet person like Mary.

With its power source finally severed, the monster machine clicked and clacked as it tried desperately to munch its last frames of film. With one last groan, it died a defiant death.

While a single frame of the film was projected onto the off-white screen, the bulb of the projector slowly faded to black. And the machine, as well as the room, went dark.

With the machine noise stopped, the students peered up from their desks and brushed the bits of film off of their clothes. Bobby Aaron moaned from under his desk and rubbed his shin.

Nick snored.

"Will someone please turn on the lights?" the teacher asked wearily.

Tammy James reached over and felt the wall in compliance. Feeling the wall plate, she flicked on the switch.

At that exact moment, the hot bulb buried deep inside the devil machine's heart exploded with a loud "POP!" and a flash of smoke and flame.

As any A/V tech knows, you must run the fan for at least five minutes after you turn off the bulb in order to cool it off properly. With the sudden loss of power, the bulb had cooled off too quickly and, unable to adjust to the sudden change in temperature, exploded—or possibly imploded . . . But whatever it did, it happened precisely at the moment that Tammy James turned the lights on, which convinced her that the lights and the explosion were in some sort of cause-and-affect relationship.

So she turned the lights back off.

Which made the scene in the middle of the room even more dramatic.

The projector was on fire.

"Fire!" somebody yelled and headed for the hallway.

"Get a fire extinguisher!" the teacher yelled at everybody and nobody.

"And turn the lights back on!" he yelled at Tammy James.

Tammy, still convinced she had caused the explosion, would have nothing to do with the wall switch.

Over by the projector, Nick finally opened one eye, saw the flames and felt the bits of film on his skin. Still half asleep, it didn't take much for Nick to convince himself that a swarm of ants had taken him hostage and that the entire bunch of them were going to be lit on fire by some pyromaniac kid.

Karl George pushed Tammy away from the light switches and turned the lights on just as Nick jumped up from his desk trying to rid himself of the "ants" while he yelled, "Don't do it! Don't do it! I don't want to burn!"

This of course convinced Tammy that the lights were somehow causing Nick to catch on fire, just like they did the projector. With a shove that belied her small size, Tammy pushed Karl away from the light switches and promptly turned the lights back off.

At that moment, Tommy Doyle returned from the hall with the fire extinguisher, only to find that the small fire that had erupted from the projector had already died out.

Not wanting it to erupt again, or more importantly, not wanting to miss the chance to legally discharge a fire extinguisher in school, Tommy doused the projector with a lethal dose of fire-stopping CO_2.

Well, actually, he doused what he thought was the projector with a lethal dose of fire stopping CO_2.

He was actually dousing the slumped over form of Bobby Aaron, who promptly screamed a scream that eclipsed the pitch and frequency of his other screams by an exponential factor of two.

On his way home from school that afternoon, Dean reached into his pocket and pulled out a single frame of film.

He started to throw it away, but decided to keep it as a memento of the day instead.

Then he studied the piece in an effort to see if he could tell what part of the film it came from.

It was a single picture of a man in a white coat facing the camera.

The man appeared to be pointing off screen. Dean tried to imagine what he was pointing at, but without the rest of the film, he would never know.

Years later, when he was writing his thesis for his Ph.D., Dean would use that piece of film as a prime example that life was a movie, not snapshot.

A movie with millions and millions of pictures and words.

And just like that one frame of film could not tell the entire movie; one snapshot from our lives cannot tell what is truly going on.

The minute a picture is taken, it's history. Life changes even in the time it takes to look at the picture.

A lot of people take snapshots of today and hold on to them as if they will still be true tomorrow.

They won't be.

Life is a movie.

Just like a film that is made up of thousands of snapshots and fed through the projector one at a time, we have millions of snapshots that are being fed through our lives. To take any one of those snapshots (the day you were born, the day you graduated, this moment right now as you read this book) and say that the rest of your life will forever be the same as the moment captured in that snapshot would be ridiculous.

It is easy to take a snapshot of our situation today and become depressed as we become convinced that the rest of our life will be the same.

It won't be.

Life is a movie, not a snapshot.

Don't freeze-frame your life as it is.

Or, to say it positively . . .

Negatives become positives over time.

"It is never too late to be what you might have been."
—George Eliot

Students of the Italian teacher Maria Montessori contend that she changed the lives of poor children when she gave them "meaningful work."

Not just work, but *meaningful* work.

As I have thought about that phrase, I have come to the conclusion that if one does not have "meaningful work" it is virtually impossible to be a positive person.

The number of successful businessmen, actors and musicians who kill themselves every year is proof enough to me that fame and fortune is simply not enough to get people through tough times—and tough times show up on every single person's doorstep . . . regardless of how much or how little money someone makes.

What is "meaningful work"? Simply put, if you'd do your work for free, it's probably meaningful work.

If your job is not the "meaningful work" that feeds your soul, maybe it's time to let go of it. Training for a new job can be very meaningful. Or maybe a huge change isn't what's needed. In that case, "meaningful work" can be something as simple as a hobby or as deep as family, faith or charity.

It doesn't matter.

Just make sure that you have enough meaningful work in your life.

And here is the best part: *You* get to decide what's meaningful. It doesn't make any difference what you choose, as long as it's productive, helpful or engaging. With meaningful work, you will find a reason to get up in the morning and feel good about yourself when you go to bed.

If you're worried that you don't have time to make changes, always remember: *THE GAME IS LONGER THAN YOU THINK.* I know of one billionaire who started his business after the age of 55.

If you don't know which direction to go, just get started. *MOVE ON.* It's easier to turn a truck when it's moving than when it's standing still.

If you've tried things in the past and have let fear affect the outcome, keep in mind that *FEAR CAN'T CHANGE THE*

WEATHER. Fear is a valid emotion; just don't live there. Slow down, think things through and take the best path.

If you've failed in the past, remember Nine-Ball billiards: *THE FIRST EIGHT BALLS DON'T COUNT.*

But most importantly, realize that if you want something to change, *YOU HAVE TO GIVE UP SOMETHING TO GET SOMETHING.* If all you want is for other people to change to suit you, it probably won't happen.

LIFE IS A MOVIE, not a snapshot. The only time the movie stops is when the film breaks or the movie ends. If you feel like your movie is broken, don't succumb to being *SOAKED WITH SADNESS.* There are things working in your favor that you can't even see.

It's OK to *GIVE IN*; just don't give up.

And remember, even if it seems as if all hope is lost, there's *A RAFT AROUND THE CORNER* that you can't even imagine.

When things aren't going well and we look into the future, we tend to see the worst possible outcome. That's OK. If you are walking through the woods and you don't even allow yourself to *think* about the bears in the woods, you could find yourself on the business end of a bear's shish-kabob. (I know bears don't cook shish-kabobs, but I like to let my imagination loose now and then.)

Negative thoughts are not the problem, negative actions are.

When we give up, we make a negative outcome inevitable.

When we keep working, we make a positive outcome *possible*.

And when we keep working *after* a negative outcome, we make a positive outcome *inevitable*.

All you have to do is keep working . . . and you'll find yourself in the right place at the right time.

There are amazing things—things that are better than you could ever imagine—and they are just waiting to float around the corner into your life.

There's a raft around the corner.

Comments?

david@araftaroundthecorner.com

For audio versions of this book
or to see if there is a book signing in your area:

www.araftaroundthecorner.com